¿Dónde está querido dragón?

Where is Dear Dragon?

por/by Margaret Hillert
ilustrado por/Illustrated by David Schimmell

NORWOOD HOUSE  PRESS

Queridos padres y maestros:

La serie para lectores principiantes es una colección de lecturas cuidadosamente escritas, muchas de las cuales ustedes recordarán de su propia infancia. Cada libro comprende palabras de uso frecuente en español e inglés y, a través de la repetición, le ofrece al niño la oportunidad de practicarlas. Los detalles adicionales de las ilustraciones refuerzan la historia y le brindan la oportunidad de ayudar a su niño a desarrollar el lenguaje oral y la comprensión.

Primero, léale el cuento al niño; después deje que él lea las palabras con las que está familiarizado y pronto, podrá leer solito todo el cuento. En cada paso, elogie el esfuerzo del niño para que se sienta más confiado como lector independiente. Hable sobre las ilustraciones y anime al niño a relacionar el cuento con su propia vida.

Sobre todo, la parte más importante de la experiencia de la lectura es ¡divertirse y disfrutarla!

Shannon Cannon

Shannon Cannon
Consultora de lectoescritura

Dear Caregiver,

The *Beginning-to-Read* series is a carefully written collection of readers, many of which you may remember from your own childhood. This book, *Dear Dragon's Day with Father*, was written over 30 years after the first *Dear Dragon* books were published. The *New Dear Dragon* series features the same elements of the earlier books, such as text comprised of common sight words. These sight words provide your child with ample practice reading the words that appear most frequently in written text. The many additional details in the pictures enhance the story and offer the opportunity for you to help your child expand oral language skills and develop comprehension.

Begin by reading the story to your child, followed by letting him or her read familiar words and soon your child will be able to read the story independently. At each step of the way, be sure to praise your reader's efforts to build his or her confidence as an independent reader. Discuss the pictures and encourage your child to make connections between the story and his or her own life.

Above all, the most important part of the reading experience is to have fun and enjoy it!

Shannon Cannon

Shannon Cannon,
Literacy Consultant

Norwood House Press • P.O. Box 316598 • Chicago, Illinois 60631
For more information about Norwood House Press please visit our website at
www.norwoodhousepress.com or call 866-565-2900.
Text copyright ©2014 by Margaret Hillert. Illustrations and cover design copyright ©2014 by
Norwood House Press, Inc. All rights reserved. No part of this book may be reproduced or utilized
in any form or by any means without written permission from the publisher.
Designer: The Design Lab

LIBRARY OF CONGRESS CATALOGING-IN-PUBLICATION DATA
 Hillert, Margaret.
  ¿Dónde está querido dragón? = Where is dear dragon? / por Margaret Hillert
 ; ilustrado por David Schimmell ; traducido por Queta Fernandez.
    pages cm. -- (A beginning-to-read book)
  Summary: "A boy looks in all types of places inside and out for his
 missing dragon"-- Provided by publisher.
  ISBN 978-1-59953-615-6 (library edition : alk. paper) -- ISBN
 978-1-60357-623-9 (ebook)
 [1. Hide-and-seek--Fiction. 2. Dragons--Fiction. 3. Spanish language
 materials--Bilingual.] I. Schimmell, David, illustrator. II. Fernandez,
 Queta, translator. III. Hillert, Margaret. ¿Dónde está querido dragón?
 Spanish. IV. Hillert, Margaret. Where is dear dragon? V. Title. VI. Title:
 Where is dear dragon?
  PZ73.H557203 2014
  [E]--dc23
                                    2013034960

Manufactured in the United States of America in Brainerd, Minnesota.
240N—012014

¿Dónde estás, querido dragón?
¿Estás en esta casita roja?
Sal de ahí.
Sal de ahí.

Where are you, Dear Dragon?
Are you in this little red house?
Come out.
Come out.

No, no estás ahí.
Mamá, mamá.
No puedo encontrar a querido dragón.
¿Dónde puede estar?

No, you are not there.
Mother. Mother.
I cannot find Dear Dragon.
Where can he be?

No lo vi.
Tendrás que buscarlo.

I did not see him.
You will have to look for him.

Aquí voy. Oh, oh.
Puedo buscar a dragón en esta caja grande.

Here I go. Oh, oh.
I can look for Dragon in this big box.

7

Mira aquí.
Aquí está mi pelota azul.

Look here.
Here is my blue ball.

8

Y aquí hay un bate rojo
y una gorra amarilla,
¡pero no está querido dragón!

And here is a red bat.
And a yellow hat.
But—no Dear Dragon!

9

También puedo buscar aquí.
¿Está dragón aquí?
Quiero encontrar a ese dragón.

I can look in here, too.
Is Dragon in here?
I want that dragon.

No, no.
No está aquí.
¿Dónde puede estar?

No, no.
He is not in here.
Where can he be?

Hay otro lugar.
Lo buscaré allí.
¿Lo encontraré?

Now there is a spot.
I will look there.
Will I find him there?

No, no está dragón.

No, no Dragon.

Afuera, afuera.
Ahora voy a salir a buscar a dragón.

Out. Out.
Now I will go out to look for Dragon.

¿Estás aquí afuera?
¿Saliste?
Quiero encontrarte.

Are you out here now?
Did you come out here?
I want you.

¿Estas aquí, dragón?
¿Te subiste al carro?
No, ya veo que no.

Are you in here, Dragon?
Did you get into the car?
No, I guess not.

19

¿Encontró mamá a dragón?
Iré a ver.
Entraré a la casa para ver.

Did Mother find Dragon for me?
I will go and see.
I will go into the house and see.

No, no vi a dragón.

No I did not see Dragon.

¡Aaayyy! ¿Bajaste para acá?
Sube. Sube.

Oooohhh! Did you go down here?
Come up. Come up.

No puedo encontrar a dragón.

I cannot find Dragon.

Mamá, mamá.

No puedo encontrar a dragón.

¿Me lo encontraste?

Mother. Mother.

I cannot find Dragon.

Did you find him for me?

Ven aquí ahora.

Tenemos trabajo que hacer.

Puedes hacer tu cama.

Come here now.

We have work to do

You can make the be

Oh, oh.
¿Qué es esto?
¿Qué hay en mi cama?

Oh, oh.
What is this?
What is in my bed?

¡TÚ!
Estás aquí, dragón.
¡Estás en mi cama!

YOU!
Here you are Dragon.
You are in my bed!

Ahora tú estás conmigo
y yo estoy contigo.
Qué querido dragón tan y tan divertido.

Now here you are with me.
And here I am with you.
What a funny, funny dear dragon.

READING REINFORCEMENT

The following activities support the findings of the National Reading Panel that determined the most effective components for reading instruction are: Phonemic Awareness, Phonics, Vocabulary, Fluency, and Text Comprehension.

Phonemic Awareness: The /w/ Sound

Sound Substitution: Say the words on the left to your child. Ask your child to repeat the word, changing the first sound to /w/:

talk = walk	me = we	pill = will	pay = way
mall= wall	cake = wake	save = wave	tag = wag
bear = wear	pin = win	dish = wish	poke = woke
nest = west	need = weed	paste = waste	bait = wait

Phonics: The letter Ww

1. Demonstrate how to form the letters **W** and **w** for your child.

2. Have your child practice writing **W** and **w** at least three times each.

3. Ask your child to point to the words in the book that start with the letter **w**.

4. Write down the following words and ask your child to circle the letter **w** in each word:

we	who	work	paw	with	cow	crawl
well	will	throw	what	walk	tower	low

Vocabulary: Story Words

1. Write the following words on sticky note paper and point to them as you read them to your child:

    house bat ball hat car bed

2. Mix the words up. Say each word in random order and ask your child to point to the correct word as you say it.

3. Mix the words up and ask your child to read as many as he or she can.

4. Ask your child to place the sticky notes on the correct page for each word that describes something in the story.

5. Say the following sentences aloud and ask your child to point to the word that is described:

- A _____ is where people live and has a roof. (house)
- Soccer is a sport played with a _____. (ball)
- You can wear a _____ on your head. (hat)
- A ____ has four wheels and an engine. (car)
- Baseball players use a _____ to hit homeruns. (bat)
- You sleep in a _____. (bed)

Fluency: Choral Reading

1. Reread the story with your child at least two more times while your child tracks the print by running a finger under the words as they are read. Ask your child to read the words he or she knows with you.

2. Reread the story aloud together. Be careful to read at a rate that your child can keep up with.

3. Repeat choral reading and allow your child to be the lead reader and ask him or her to change from a whisper to a loud voice while you follow along and change your voice.

Text Comprehension: Discussion Time

1. Ask your child to retell the sequence of events in the story.

2. To check comprehension, ask your child the following questions:

- Where were some places the boy looked for Dear Dragon?
- What did the boy find in his toy box?
- Where did the boy find Dear Dragon?
- How do you think the boy felt on page 28 when he found Dear Dragon?
- What was your favorite part of the story? Why?

Margaret Hillert ha escrito más de 80 libros para niños que están aprendiendo a leer. Sus libros han sido traducidos a muchos idiomas y han sido leídos por más de un millón de niños de todo el mundo. De niña, Margaret empezó escribiendo poesía y más adelante siguió escribiendo para niños y adultos. Durante 34 años, fue maestra de primer grado. Ya se retiró, y ahora vive en Michigan donde le gusta escribir, dar paseos matinales y cuidar a sus tres gatos.

Photograph by Glenna Washburn

Margaret Hillert has written over 80 books for children who are just learning to read. Her books have been translated into many different languages and over a million children throughout the world have read her books. She first started writing poetry as a child and has continued to write for children and adults throughout her life. A first grade teacher for 34 years, Margaret is now retired from teaching and lives in Michigan where she likes to write, take walks in the morning, and care for her three cats.

David Schimmell fue bombero durante 23 años, al cabo de los cuales guardó las botas y el casco y se dedicó a trabajar como ilustrador. David ha creado las ilustraciones para la nueva serie de Querido dragón, así como para muchos otros libros. David nació y se crió en Evansville, Indiana, donde aún vive con su esposa, dos hijos, un nieto y dos nietas.

David Schimmell served as a professional firefighter for 23 years before hanging up his boots and helmet to devote himself to work as an illustrator. David has happily created the illustrations for the New Dear Dragon books as well as many other books throughout his career. Born and raised in Evansville, Indiana, he lives there today with his wife, two sons, a grandson and two granddaughters.

32